LONG CLAWS

AN ARCTIC ADVENTURE

LONG CLAWS

AN ARCTIC ADVENTURE

WRITTEN & ILLUSTRATED BY

JAMES HOUSTON

McCLELLAND AND STEWART

Songs of the Dream People:
Chants and Images from the Indians and Eskimos
of North America
Kiviok's Magic Journey: An Eskimo Legend
Frozen Fire: A Tale of Courage
River Runners: A Tale of Hardship and Bravery

All rights reserved
The Canadian Publishers
McClelland and Stewart Limited
25 Hollinger Road, Toronto M4B 3G2

Canadian Cataloguing in Publication Data

Houston, James, 1921-
  Long claws
ISBN 0-7710-4256-6
I. Title
PS8515.086L66   jC813'.54   C81-094442-1
PZ7.H68Lo

Composed by American-Stratford Graphic Services, Inc.
Brattleboro, Vermont
Manufactured by Halliday Lithograph Corporation
West Hanover, Massachusetts
Designed by Maria Epes
Published simultaneously in the United States by Atheneum Publishers
Manufactured in the United States of America

To my goddaughter, Susan Echalook,
her mother, Uvilu,
and her grandmother, Echalook

ᐸᓂᔪᐊᓄᑦ ᓯᓴᐊ ᐃᖃᖬᔪᖅ
ᐊᓇᓇᒃᖬᖏᓄ ᐅᕕᓗᑎᐦ
ᐊᓇᕐᓯᐊᖅᖭᒥᓄ ᐃᖃᖬᖅᖬᑎᐦ
ᓴᐃᓯᒥ

Pitohok and Upik hurried back into the igloo, shouting, "An owl helped us! Look! We found these fish where it scratched the snow. We dug them up. Four big ones!" Upik clutched the frozen lake trout in her arms, displaying them like precious silver toys. Someone had buried them outside to be eaten later.

Upik handed the largest trout to her mother, who held it over the small flame of her stone lamp until it softened slightly.

"I treasure my hunger before a feast," she whispered as she passed the fish and her sharp-curved ulu knife around to the other members of the family. She gazed at her four children— Pitohok and Upik, their small sister Kanajuk and the baby, who was peeking out from the hood of her parka. Then she looked at her old father. Would any of them survive now that her husband was no longer living?

Pitohok, her son, had a smooth brown face and quick, dark eyes. His teeth were square and strong. Like his sister, he wore a fur parka and pants and boots made of caribou skins. Bundled up like that, they both looked plump. Only the dark shadows below their broad cheekbones betrayed their hunger.

7

Upik's black shiny eyes, white teeth, and wide, clear face were a pleasure to see. When her parka hood was pushed back, her lustrous blue-black hair hung down in two braids thickened by willow sticks and bound stiff with beads.

When the grandfather sniffed the rich smell of thawing fish, he sat up slowly on the fur-covered sleeping platform that was made of snow. Quickly, they each ate their share of the fish.

"Grandfather," Pitohok said, "the fish will give us enough strength to travel. Tell me where the last caribou is buried so that I may go and find it."

"Oh, it is far from here," his grandfather answered. "Too great a distance for you to go alone."

Pitohok looked at his sister and wondered if she had enough strength to walk with him on such a journey.

"Tell me where it lies," Pitohok asked again.

"It is three days' hard walking west of here," his grandfather said, "near the short hill that stands before the Crooked River. Out on that plain last autumn a young male caribou fell before my rifle. A strong wind was blowing and it began to snow. A great feeling of weakness came over me. I had no way to carry home that last caribou and no time to build a proper cache to hide it. I knew that the heavy snows would drift over its body, hiding all but its horns from sight. So I turned its antlers high hoping that someone might find it later." He looked at Pitohok. "It is too great a journey for one person without dogs."

"I will go with him," said Upik.

"Yes, she could help him," said their mother.

Their grandfather closed his eyes in pain. "It is our only chance. If you two make such a journey, you must first search for the Crooked River. Beyond it stands the pointed hill. If you find that hill, climb to its peak and carefully study the land. I believe that you will see that caribou's antlers standing wind-

blown, clear of snow. It is bad that we had to break up the sled and burn its wood in the coldest days of winter. It is sad that the dogs are gone," he said. "But it is good that we are all alive! I will try hard to think of some way to make a sled for you."

"We will need to dig for that caribou," Pitohok said, "but we cannot find the shovel."

"Of course, you cannot find the snow shovel," their grandfather said. "I warned all of you that that shovel should have been left lying flat. Someone in this camp stood it upright in the snow. I saw it," the old man said. "It was standing like a human. That shovel has a soul like any one of us, like birds, like caribou, like fish, like every other thing. When someone left it standing, it did just what you or I would do. As soon as it grew dark, that shovel ran away. Why not? It doesn't like to stand out there in the cold waiting to be a slave to any one of us!"

Pitohok and his sister did not pause long to puzzle over their grandfather's old-fashioned ideas. Hunger made them think only of food. They were desperate. No one in their family had eaten anything save that single fish for six long days.

Upik looked into her mother's eyes. She could see hunger there and fear that the caribou herds, which were their main food, would not come again in time to save their lives.

"Sleep well," their mother told them. "Only tomorrow when your grandfather looks at the sky will it be decided whether you will go or stay."

"If you cannot find the shovel," their grandfather told Pitohok, "take the hand axe and my old snow knife. You can dig with them."

That night the grandfather asked Pitohok's mother to soak two caribou skins in water. When she had done this, he carefully folded each of them lengthwise six times and turned them up on the ends until they took on the rough appearance of a pair of sled runners. These he placed outside to freeze.

Upik's mother stayed awake sewing by her lamp throughout the night so that she could give her two older children each a pair of warm, new caribou-skin boots. In the morning the wind was down, but it was bitter cold.

"Bring in the frozen runners," said the grandfather. "If they are hard enough, I shall show you how to build a small sled, using only what we have."

The old man examined the two frozen skins that he had so carefully shaped into sled runners. They were straight and not much longer than his outstretched arms. They were frozen as hard as wood.

Taking an old-fashioned bowdrill, the grandfather placed between his teeth a small bone with a hole in it, shaped just large and deep enough to hold one end of the arrowlike drill shaft. He twisted the string of a short bow around this shaft. By

10

drawing the short bow swiftly back and forth with his right hand in a sawing motion, he made the shaft whirl around so that the sharp nail in its lower end became a drill. Pressing hard, he drilled three holes near the top of each folded caribou-skin runner and forced strong braided caribou sinew through each of these holes.

"Hand me those last three frozen fish," the old man said.

Pitohok passed them to his grandfather.

The grandfather carefully lashed the three stiffly frozen trout on top of the runners so they would serve as cross bars. In this way he was able to bind together a sturdy makesift sled.

"Now hand me those pulling straps," he said to Upik's mother.

He drilled two more holes in the runners and attached the long leather straps to the front of the sled. Pitohok stood before him while he adjusted this harness to fit Pitohok's shoulders.

"Now," said their grandfather, "here is my old rifle and the only two brass cartridges left to us. I have loaded these with the last two pinches of gunpowder we possess. We have no more lead to make bullets, so I have carved two bullets of stone to fit into these cartridge casings. Stone bullets are strong enough, but I must warn you that they sometimes break and fly apart. Go with strength." Their grandfather sighed. "If you can find that buried caribou, we may all live to see the summer come again."

Upik and Pitohok pulled on their warmest clothing and tied up a roll of caribou sleeping skins.

"We won't come back until we have the meat," Pitohok told his grandfather.

Upik and Pitohok bent low as they went out the long snow tunnel that protected their igloo from the Arctic winds. Their mother followed them outside, but they could find no words to say between them. She held Kanajuk's hand as she watched Upik and Pitohok trudge away, dragging the small frozen sled behind them. Tears filled her eyes, for she wondered whether she would ever see her children again.

Beyond the igloo, the vast flat white snow plain stretched all around them. Far to the east lay Hudson Bay, to the south frozen Kasba Lake. To the north and west the land continued endlessly toward distant, blue, snow-covered mountains and oceans that they had never seen.

Upik and Pitohok traveled steadily westward. The late winter sun faded and soon the whole sky was hidden by a heavy blanket of gray clouds that stretched to the far horizons of the enormous snow-covered land. Only the painful squeal of snow beneath their soft skin boots broke the silence that hung around them.

As it grew dark, the first snowflakes floated down from the western sky. Then gusts of wind swept moaning across the land, driving the fine snow upward into whirling, twisting forms that drifted toward them, then scurried away like ghosts across the lonely plain.

12

Pitohok stopped at once and drew the snow knife from beneath the lashings of the sled. He licked both sides of the long thin antler blade until it was glazed with ice and would slice smoothly into the hard snow beneath his feet. Carefully he cut out snow blocks and stood them around him in a small circle, cleverly piling them until they curved in at the top to form a dome. Upik stayed outside and packed dry snow into the chinks between the blocks. She could feel the cold wind's force increasing and knew that any weakness in their igloo might allow it to be broken and torn to pieces. Their house of snow was just big enough for the two of them. Upik wondered if it would stand firm.

She stuffed their caribou sleeping robes through the low entrance, and Pitohok yelled to her against the howling wind, "Push the sled inside as well. We may have to eat it before this storm has ended."

He was right. The blizzard raged and screamed over their small shelter for three long, gloomy days and terrifying nights, leaving them weak with fear and hunger. Their igloo trembled like a frightened rabbit during the awful storm. But it held.

On the fourth morning the wind died out. Pitohok looked at the three frozen trout that formed their small sled. "Tomorrow we will have to eat one of the fish, or we will not have the strength to travel. Two fish will be just enough to hold the sled together."

That night Upik unlashed the lake trout that had been the sled's center crossbar and placed it between herself and the caribou robe beneath her. She slept on top of it all night. In the morning her body heat had thawed the fish enough for them to eat. They shared it with the eagerness of wild animals.

All that day they traveled, then built another igloo and slept again. When they crawled out at dawn, Pitohok pointed into the west. "Do you see something strange over there?"

He cupped his mittened hands together and boosted his sister high. She shaded her eyes and examined the flat horizon.

"It's the hill!" she cried. "And beyond it I can see a long windswept streak that looks like ice. That must be the Crooked River."

"Hurry," said Pitohok. "We must find that caribou while the light is strong."

It was almost evening when they reached the pointed hill. It was not much taller than two men standing one on the shoulders of the other, but in this dead-flat land it looked like an enormous mountain. Eagerly Pitohok climbed it. As he reached the top, he disturbed a snowy owl that took flight across the plain.

Upik, seeing it, crouched down and sang her secret song:

> "White owl, I sing to you.
> Softly I sing to you,
> Owl, my helping spirit."

"Look! Look out there where she is flying," called Pitohok. I can see the caribou antlers standing upright in the snow. But do you see something moving toward the antlers through the blue shadows of the snowdrift?"

15

"Yes, I see it," Upik called up to him. "It's dark brown and humped over like a dog."

"It's Kugvik, the wolverine!" said Pitohok. "Look at the way that one moves and digs. They're the worst meat robbers in the world. Quick! I need the rifle."

Upik untied their grandfather's old rifle from the sled and carried it up to her brother. Pitohok sat down on the snow. From his small leather bag, he took out the two precious brass cartridges and examined the stone bullets. He chose one, opened the rifle, and placed the cartridge in its breech.

He held his grandfather's heavy rifle steady by resting his elbows on his knees. With one eye closed, he took careful aim at the wolverine that was digging with its sharp claws through the hard-packed snow, trying to get at the caribou.

Upik jumped back as the heavy rifle boomed and echoed across the wide snow plain.

"I missed," said Pitohok, his voice full of disappointment.

16

"That's no wonder," Upik called to him. "The bullet that you fired broke into three small pieces. I saw the bits of stone fall onto the snow. But the noise of the rifle frightened the wolverine. He is running away!"

Pitohok came leaping down the hill and lashed the rifle onto the sled again. "Follow me!" he said, snatching up the long straps. "We must reach that caribou before night comes."

The first stars twinkled in the western sky as they came up to the caribou antlers that stood above the snow.

Pitohok stared in wonder at his sister. "Is that grandfather's shovel standing in the snow beside the antlers?" he whispered. "Are we seeing something magic?"

"Is it truly ours?" asked Upik.

"Yes, it's ours," said Pitohok, bending to look closely at its familiar wooden shape and its worn leather stitching. "I'd know that snow shovel anywhere. I've dug with it so many times."

"Grandfather must have left it here last autumn," Upik said, "when he was growing weak and it was dark and storming."

Pitohok drew the snow knife from beneath the lashings of the sled and paced out a circle for their igloo.

"I am going to build it right on top of the caribou, leaving only its horns outside," Pitohok said, "so that wolverines can't come back here in the night and steal the meat from us."

When their new igloo was completed, Upik looked up and saw the cold-faced winter moon rising in the eastern sky. As Pitohok crawled into the igloo, he sighed and said, "Perhaps we don't have to eat. My belly feels full just knowing that we're going to sleep on top of all this rich caribou meat." He patted their snow floor. "Imagine how glad our family will be when we return with such a treasure."

They rose early in the morning and tried again to forget their hunger as they broke the igloo's side walls. Using the snow knife and the shovel, they dug up the frozen caribou and lashed it onto the small sled.

Before they left, Pitohok carefully stood the shovel upright in the snow. He smiled and said, "If you can walk, please hurry home to our grandfather and tell him we are coming."

The snow shovel did not move or seem to hear his words.

Pitohok took up the long pulling straps and together they headed back toward their home. They hauled the welcome weight of meat behind them, following their own footprints eastward, hurrying until it was almost dark. Then they built a small igloo and slept exhausted.

Many times the following morning Upik looked back at the precious caribou lashed to the creaking sled. She tried to fight off her hunger by saying, "Just think of the wonderful smell that meat will make as it simmers in our mother's pot."

The morning sun had risen high above the plain when Pitohok stopped and pushed up his wooden goggles. He shaded his eyes,

18

then pointed at a small dark speck far away. "Do you see it?"

"Yes, what is it?" Upik asked him as she watched it moving slowly toward them across the endless plain of snow.

"I don't know," said Pitohok as he pulled down his goggles to protect his eyes again. "It's not a caribou or a man. But it is certainly something that's alive."

"Let us hurry home," said Upik. "I don't like the look of that moving spot. It sways from side to side in a heavy way that frightens me."

By midafternoon the brown speck had grown much larger.

"It is moving faster than we can walk. What is it?" Upik asked her brother.

"I am not sure," he said, handing her one of the straps. "Let us run for a little while together, then walk, and run again. Perhaps it will turn and go away."

In the late afternoon they had to stop and rest because their legs were too tired to go on.

"Can you tell now what it is," Upik asked, "that thing that is coming closer to us?"

"Yes," Pitohok said. "It is Akla, a barren-ground grizzly bear. It is moving in our footprints, following our scent."

"I am afraid," said Upik. "I have never seen an akla, but I have heard terrible things about them. Hunters call them 'Long Claws.' "

"Let us walk fast again," said Pitohok.

When the sun started to sink into the west, Pitohok knew that they could not get away from the huge, hump-shouldered grizzly that came shambling after them, rolling its enormous hips, gaining on them with every step it took.

"We've got to do something," Pitohok gasped, and now his voice was full of fear. "That akla's going to catch us no matter how fast we walk. And if we run now, it may get excited and attack. Grizzlies are tireless in following their prey and can make short, fast bursts of speed. Grandfather has told me that strong aklas in their prime can sometimes catch a running caribou."

"What shall we do?" Upik asked him, and Pitohok could tell by her voice that she was almost crying.

Pitohok stopped and drew his grandfather's rifle out from under the sled lashings. He put their last stone-nosed cartridge inside its barrel. Looking at his sister, he said, "I hope we won't have to use it."

He stood the rifle upright in the snow. Then quickly he bent and unlashed the frozen caribou and rolled it off the sled. With his short, sharp knife he cut the bindings that held the sled together. As it fell apart, Pitohok grabbed one of the runners. Whirling it around his head, he threw it as far as he could along the trail toward the oncoming grizzly. The second runner he flung far to the right, hoping to draw the big bear away from their path.

The akla stopped, raised its massive head and stared at the two human creatures. Pitohok and Upik could hear its stomach rumbling with hunger as it ambled forward and sniffed the folded caribou skin. Placing one paw upon it, the grizzly tore it into pieces with its teeth and began devouring it.

Pitohok knelt down beside the frozen caribou and grasped it by its front and rear legs. "Quick!" he said to Upik. "Help me heave this meat onto my shoulders."

She did so, scarcely able to believe how heavy it was.

As soon as Pitohok rose to his feet, he started walking, hurrying once more along their own trail that would lead them home.

"You bring the rifle and the snow knife and the last two fish," he called back to his sister. One sleeping robe will have to do us. Tie it around yourself. Leave the other one. Move!" Upik could hear a sound of horror creeping into his voice again. "Don't let that Long Claws near you!"

Upik's legs ached with tiredness, but she hurried after him, afraid to look back, afraid she would find the grizzly close behind her.

The evening sun turned red as it slid down and touched the long, flat white horizon. Pitohok looked back then and groaned beneath the heavy weight of caribou. "Long Claws is still coming after us. Give him a fish. Hurry and fling it back toward him."

Upik did as she was told. Pitohok looked again, then slowed his pace. "He's lying down," Pitohok gasped. "He's eaten the trout. He looks now as if he's going to sleep." It was growing dark and Pitohok was staggering with weariness. "Hold onto me," he groaned. "Help me. I've got to make my feet carry me over that next snow ridge so the akla won't see us stop to build our igloo."

When they were beyond the huge bear's sight, Pitohok collapsed, letting the caribou fall to the snow. Upik helped him up, but Pitohok was so exhausted that he could scarcely rise. With the snow knife Upik cut a shallow gravelike hole and they slid the caribou in and carefully covered it with snow. They built their igloo on top of it.

Once inside, Pitohok wedged a snow block firmly into place, trying to jam the entrance. "Let us share our one last fish," he said. "I have never been so hungry or so tired in all my life."

Even while they were eating, they listened carefully. But they did not hear the akla. Upik could not finish her share of the fish, so exhausted was she from their terrible journey. They rolled themselves into the caribou robe and slept, not knowing if the akla would let them live to see the next day dawn.

When Pitohok awoke, he said, "The weather's changed. Can you not smell and feel spring's dampness in the air?"

Cautiously he cut away the entrance block and crawled outside. Upik followed him. The land was blanketed in lead-gray fog that hung heavily above the snow, hiding everything from view. The huge akla might have been very close to them or very far away.

Pitohok dug up the caribou and cutting a larger entrance in their igloo, shoved the frozen animal outside.

"There is Long Claws. He is waiting for us," Upik whispered with terror in her voice.

Pitohok looked up and saw the dark outline of the akla standing watching them. It was less than a stone's throw away, its wide back glistening with silver hoarfrost, which made the coarse hair on its massive shoulders bristle like countless needles.

"Shall I try to shoot him now?" Pitohok whispered to his sister.

"No," she said. "No! I'm afraid that last bullet will break and the noise will only anger him."

"Then hurry," he cried. "Help me get this caribou up onto my back. I don't know how far I can carry it today. My legs feel weak as water. But we've got to get it home."

Swaying its huge head back and forth, the grizzly let a low growl rumble in its throat. It was so close now that for the first time Upik could see the akla's long, sharp claws. They cut deep furrows in the snow when it came shambling toward them. Its beady black eyes watched every move they made.

"Leave our caribou sleeping skin in front of the igloo. That may fool him," Pitohok whispered. "If he goes inside, he will surely smell the place where the caribou lay last night. He may stay there digging long enough for us to lose him."

Together they hurried away, trying to hide themselves from Long Claws in the heavy ice fog. They walked and walked until they came to a riverbed that seemed familiar to them. Violent winds had blown one bank free of snow, but in the swirling fog they could not tell where it would lead them. Pitohok struggled up onto the stones that formed the bank of the frozen river. His sister had to help him by pushing at his back.

"Be careful not to leave a single track up here," Pitohok gasped. "Step from rock to rock," he warned her. "The wind is at our back. If the akla cannot see us or smell our footprints, we may lose him."

Together they traveled on the stony river bank until about midday, following a twisted course, leaving no path behind them.

"I hope we are far enough away from him," Pitohok gasped. "I can walk no farther."

He sank to his knees and let the heavy weight of the caribou sag down until it rested on the wind-cleared stones. He lay against it, his chest heaving as he tried to catch his breath. Although the air was stinging cold, Upik had to kneel and wipe the frost-white sweat from her brother's face.

"He's gone." Upik sighed, glad to rest the heavy rifle in the snow. She looked around in the still-thick fog. "Which way do we go now?"

Pitohok peered over his shoulder and felt cold sweat trickling down his spine. He could see no sign of the sun. Everything was hidden by a wall of fog.

"I . . . I don't know," he admitted. "I was trying so hard to get away from the akla that now . . . we're lost!"

Pitohok struggled painfully onto his knees and looked in all directions. He saw nothing but gray ice fog that drifted in phantom swirls along the frozen river.

"Oh, I wish someone would help us," Upik wispered aloud, and as if in answer to her words, the snowy owl came toward her, winging low out of the fog. Upik saw the owl turn its head as though it had seen the bear, then stare at her with its huge golden-yellow eyes. Suddenly the owl changed its wingbeat, hovering as if by magic at the very edge of the smokelike mists.

It seemed to signal Upik. Then, turning sharply to the right, it flew off, cutting a dark trail through the ice-cold wall of fog.

Upik stood up, and, using all her strength, helped her brother heave the caribou onto his back. She struggled to ease the heavy burden as she stood upright.

"We should follow her," said Upik. "I think she knows the way."

Her brother's answer was a moan when the full weight of the frozen caribou settled on his tired, cramped shoulders. "Yes, follow the owl," he whispered.

Upik tried to steady Pitohok while they walked. She looked back only once at the zigzag trail they left in the snow as her brother's strength grew less and less. Both of them had lost all sense of distance and of time. Upik followed the owl's course through the dense fog, wondering if they would ever reach their home.

They had not gone far before Upik heard the sound of heavy breathing. She turned, then screamed in terror. The huge griz-

zly, its heavy head rolling, its tongue lolling out of its mouth, came padding after them. It was only a pace behind Pitohok. Upik saw Long Claws raise its head and sniff at the rich burden of caribou, which had softened a little because of the heat of Pitohok's body. The grizzly stretched out its neck and licked the frosted nostrils of the caribou.

"What's the matter?" Pitohok asked her. Then turning, he, too, saw the bear. His voice caught in his throat. "You've got to . . . to try and shoot him," Pitohok gasped. "I can't do it. My arms are too tired. My whole body is trembling from carrying this weight. Let him get close to you," he said, "then shoot him . . . in the head."

Upik stopped, raised the heavy rifle and tried to sight along its wavering barrel. "I can't," she said. "I am afraid . . . afraid this last stone bullet will break." She was weeping. "Drop the caribou," Upik begged her brother. "Let Long Claws take

it. We can walk away alive. It will stop and eat. Please drop the caribou. I am afraid that the akla is going to kill you for that meat."

Pitohok hunched his shoulders and struggled forward, as if he had not heard her plea. But now Upik could see that he held his short knife in his hand and that he would not give up their prize of meat without a fight.

Once more she heard an angry rumble in the grizzly's throat and saw it reach out with one terrible paw and rake the caribou along the whole length of its back. As its claws hooked against the caribou's antlers, Pitohok was thrown off balance and stumbled sideways, falling onto his knees. The big bear moved closer. Driven by fear and desperation, Pitohok rose and continued walking, his eyes narrowed, his mouth drawn down with strain.

The huge akla, with lips drawn back to show its enormous

teeth, came after him again. Upik once more raised her grand-father's rifle and looked along its sights. The bear must have heard the safety catch click off, for it stopped, turned its head and stared straight up the gun barrel at her. At that moment, looking into its eyes, Upik realized that the bear was neither good nor evil. It was a hunter like themselves, desperate to feed itself and remain alive in the lonely, snow-filled wilderness. She lowered the rifle. She could not bring herself to try to kill the bear.

At that moment, Pitohok whispered hoarsely, "I see the owl again! She's sitting on our family's empty food cache. Can it be?" he sobbed. "Are we . . . almost home?"

The bear moved in again behind him and, raising up on its hind feet, struck out angrily at the caribou's plump haunches. Pitohok reeled from the heavy blow and staggered to his knees. He tried to rise, then sank back onto the snow.

"I can't go on," he said. "I'm finished." He had lost his knife. There were tears in his eyes, but his teeth were clenched in anger. He tightened his grip upon the caribou.

"Let go," Upik begged her brother. "Let him have the meat."

"No," Pitohok said. "If I lose this caribou to that bear and return home with nothing, none of us will live, and I, myself, would die of shame."

He turned away from the hot breath of the snarling grizzly whose great swaying head was not more than an arm's length from his face.

"Run!" Pitohok whispered to his sister. "Run for the igloo and save yourself."

Upik bent and grabbed her brother underneath the arms, trying to help him up, but he was too weak. Then she turned around so that she stood directly between him and the akla's gaping jaws.

"No—don't do that," Pitohok gasped. He was hunched over like an old man. "Put the rifle under the caribou to help me support this weight," he moaned, "or I . . . shall never rise. You run!" he begged his sister. Pitohok wept aloud as he whispered, "I can't do any more. All my strength has gone. It's going black . . . I'm going to . . ."

"You are coming with me, now!" cried Upik. "I can see our igloo. It's not far from us. Can you not see it through the fog?"

The big grizzly raked its claws through the snow. Upik put her left shoulder underneath the caribou and her arm around her brother's waist and strained with all her might. Together they rose from the snow and staggered off toward their family's house. Pitohok stumbled once again and fell onto one knee. He hung there gasping for breath.

The akla snarled and opened its mouth wide to take the caribou's leg and Pitohok's mitted hand between its crushing jaws.

"Unalook! Kukikotak!" Upik screamed at the bear. "We shared our fish with you. Don't you dare to harm my brother. He must take this food home to our family. They are starving . . . don't you understand?"

The huge bear let go of Pitohok's hand and the caribou's leg and stood there glaring back at her.

"Quick! Get back on your feet," Upik whispered. "We have only a little way to go."

The grizzly must have seen the snowhouse, too, for suddenly it shambled around in front of them, blocking Pitohok's way.

"I warned you not to hurt my brother," Upik screamed again.

As if ruled by magic, the huge bear stepped back and let them pass.

"Mother! Mother! Come and help us!" Upik wailed.

Long Claws turned its head and stared at her when Upik's mother burst out of their igloo entrance. She saw the great humped shoulders of the akla and, like her daughter, screamed at it, then turned and rushed inside again.

Upik tried to take half of the caribou's weight on her own shoulders while pulling Pitohok to his feet. Slowly he rose, but his knees would scarcely support him.

"Don't drop it now," Upik said in a stern voice. "We're almost there."

Together they staggered painfully toward the igloo.

"Everything is whirling around," cried Pitohok. "It's going black again . . . I'm falling. . . ."

Because she no longer had the strength to hold him, Upik and her brother collapsed together on the snow. She shook him, but Pitohok seemed to have lost the power to hear or move or speak. Upik tried to drag him toward the igloo, but his arms remained locked tight around their precious burden of meat.

Long Claws turned once more and shambled after them, snarling like a huge and angry dog. It grasped the caribou's neck in its powerful jaws and started backing away, dragging the carcass and Pitohok, pulling both of them into the swirling fog.

The snow knife, the rifle and Pitohok's short knife were gone. Upik had no weapons but her hands and teeth. She turned and saw her grandfather crawling out of the igloo on his hands and knees. In his left mitt he held his huge curved bow and in his mouth a pair of arrows. Right behind him came their mother, her parka hood puffed out with icy wind, screaming aloud, raging to protect her children, ready to do battle with the enormous bear. Her hands outstretched like claws, their mother raced forward to attack.

Upik heard her grandfather call out, "Stop, woman. Hold! If you help me, we can pierce him right from here."

The grandfather knelt unsteadily and notched an arrow to

the braided string. His hands shook with strain when he tried
to draw the powerful bow. But he could not. In desperation
Upik's mother knelt and helped to draw the heavy weapon
almost to full curve. The point of the arrow wavered wildly
when the grandfather tried to aim.

"Don't!" Upik cried, spreading her arms and running between her grandfather's unsteady arrow and the bear. "You
might hit Pitohok."

Looking back, she saw her brother still being dragged across
the snow behind the bear. In sudden anger she whirled around
and ran straight between her brother and the akla, screaming,
"You let go of him! Let go!"

Surprised, the huge grizzly released the caribou for a moment
and raised its head.

"Here, this is for you," she yelled and reaching into her
parka hood, she snatched out the last piece of frozen trout that
she had saved and flung it beyond the bear.

The akla looked at her, grunted, then turned and moved away from Pitohok, who still clasped the caribou as fiercely as an Arctic crab. The grizzly snatched up the piece of fish. Then, with its hips and frosted shoulders rolling, it disappeared into the silver wall of icy fog.

Pitohok's mother and his grandfather knelt beside him, trying to unlock his arms from the caribou.

Pitohok opened his eyes and stared at them. "I thought that akla would surely snatch the caribou away from me," he whispered.

"I, too, believed that he would take it from you," his grandfather agreed. "But no human knows exactly what the animals will do."

"Upik was afraid of the akla. We were both afraid of him, and yet she ran and put her body between me and the grizzly's snarling jaws. Grandfather, did you believe my sister would do that?"

"No. I did not know what she would do. Nobody knows the strength or courage that humans possess until real danger comes to test them."